Piggo has a Train Ride

Pam Ayres

Illustrations by Andy Ellis

BBC Books

Published by BBC Books,
a division of BBC Enterprises Limited,
Woodlands, 80 Wood Lane, London W12 0TT
First published 1990

Text © Pam Ayres 1990
Illustrations © Andy Ellis 1990
ISBN 0 563 20921 6

Set in Century Schoolbook by Goodfellow & Egan Ltd
Printed and bound in Great Britain by Cambus Litho Ltd, East Kilbride
Colour separations by Dot Gradations Ltd, Chelmsford
Jacket printed by Belmont Press Ltd, Northampton

Piggo the piglet lived in the Children's Farmyard at a big house called Badgerwood. Parents took their children there to spend the day and have picnics. There was a beautiful garden with fountains, an adventure playground, shops, cafes and best of all, a steam train that took the families for long rides round the whole park.

Piggo loved that steam train. It was his Favourite Thing. He loved the shiny red engine, the long plume of smoke from its funnel, the line of children laughing and waving from its red seats and the way it whistled TOOT TOOT as it bustled away on its journey.

Most of all Piggo wanted a ride on the train. But he had never had one.

One afternoon, Piggo was restless. His Mum and all his brothers and sisters had gone to sleep in a big pile in the sunshine. Piggo wasn't tired. He was just wondering what to do when he heard hooves. Round the corner came a lamb. He was white with black spots on. He jumped when he saw Piggo staring through the fence.

"Hello," he said nervously in a small voice.

"Hello," replied Piggo. "Are you new?"

"Yes," the lamb answered. "Mum and I only came this morning. I'm trying to find my way about."

"I'll show you round if you like," offered Piggo.

"Oh, thank you!" said the lamb.

Piggo told his Mum where he was going and then he and the lamb trotted off side by side.

"What's your name?" asked Piggo.

"Jacob," replied the lamb, "because I'm a Jacob sheep, you see. We have spots. What's yours?"

"Piggo," came the reply. "Mum had such a lot of piglets and I was the last and she just couldn't think of any more names. Let's go along here."

They went along the path and over a wooden bridge to the Adventure Playground.

"Look!" said Piggo excitedly.

There were tunnels to wriggle through, fat knotted ropes to swing on, ladders to climb and a wobbly suspension bridge held up with chains. The floor was covered with tiny pieces of bark so that you didn't get hurt if you fell down.

"Let's go over that bridge!" said Jacob daringly.

Together they ventured up the ramp and across the rattly bridge. Very slowly they edged their way over, feeling the bridge wobble and shake beneath their feet. They tore down the ramp at the other end and raced away squealing and bleating with excitement.

Back through the children's farmyard they galloped, shattering the peace of the afternoon. All the animals stared. Janet the Jersey cow and Dennis the donkey craned their necks to see. Edgar the shire horse woke up and blinked in surprise. Chickens, ducks and geese ran cackling in all directions and proud Mr Peacock swept away stiffly.

'What rude animals!' he declared.

Piggo and Jacob didn't hear him. By now they were racing off across the fields.

Suddenly Piggo's head snapped up. He could hear the steam train!

"Look Jacob, look! It's my Favourite Thing!" he cried and both animals watched as the red train appeared in the distance busily puffing round the grounds, streaming smoke behind it, weaving between buildings and trees, carrying children wherever they wanted to go.

They watched until it passed out of sight. Piggo felt a twinge of sadness that he could not be on it too. But Jacob was already racing up the hill, his woolly legs and black hooves flying.

Piggo gazed after him. He was getting tired. He wished *he* had long white springy legs like his new friend. But then he supposed they would look queer on a piglet. His were short and pink, and they ached. He started rather wearily up the hill.

When he reached the top, he found Jacob practising jumps, corkscrews and trying to fly. Piggo sat down beside a white fence and stared across to the Children's Farmyard where he lived. It seemed so far away. Jacob cut through the air above him, bleating for joy.

Piggo felt worried and gloomy. He had come too far. He was tired and he wanted his Mum.

TOOT TOOT! TOOT TOOT! Piggo sat up. What was that? TOOT TOOT! Piggo knew that sound! It was the steam train! Suddenly it appeared, coming merrily along the track. How smashing it looked, with its red engine shining and big puffs of smoke billowing up from the funnel. Then the brakes began to screech and the little train puffed to a halt. All the children were looking ahead as the driver called back to them:

"Here are the Highland Cattle," he was saying. "Can you see their big horns?"

A truly tremendous idea came to Piggo. Of course! The steam train could take them home!

"Come on, Jacob!" cried Piggo excitedly, forgetting how tired he was, and together they both jumped over the fence and scrambled up on to one of the red leather seats. At last! At last! A ride on the steam train he had loved for so long!

Piggo and Jacob huddled close together breathlessly as the train began to move. It gathered speed. The white fence on either side of the track began to pass more and more quickly. The air began to rush in their faces, and they could smell pine trees as the train swept down a wooded slope. Rabbits scuttled for safety. Underneath them the wheels seemed to drum out a breathless little song:

Mustn't be late, mustn't be late,
Mustn't be making the passengers wait,
Coal on the fire, smoke in the funnel,
Over the bridges and into the tunnel.

The trees flashed past and then they were out in the open. Who would have guessed it went so fast! They snaked round buildings and past fields. Everyone was waving and laughing when suddenly they were plunged into darkness! Piggo let out a little squeal of alarm, and so did many of the children.

"It's only a tunnel," said Jacob bravely. "I expect we'll be out in a minute."

They sat close together in the gloom and waited. Sure enough, a ring of bright light appeared ahead of them. It grew bigger and bigger and then they burst through it into the sunshine.

On, on went the steam train, clattering over a bridge. It was amazing to see water underneath them on both sides. Piggo and Jacob did not know where to look first, there was so much to see.

But soon the little train began to slow down. The song from the wheels grew slower and sadder and now they were passing all the places that Piggo knew best.

"Adventure Playground!" shouted the driver. "Children's Farmyard!" Gradually they came to a complete stop.

Piggo and Jacob jumped down from the train, still shaking with excitement. They stood side by side as the bright red train pulled slowly away and watched until it had disappeared. Then, hearing it whistle TOOT TOOT in the distance, Piggo and his new friend Jacob went happily home.